To Jen — D.L.

To Leigh Turina, for her warmth and encouragement — A.B.

Special thanks to Kerry Kijewski, secretary of the Ontario
chapter of the Canadian Federation of the Blind, for her
thoughtful review of the text.

Text © 2021 Darren Lebeuf
Illustrations © 2021 Ashley Barron

Published in Canada and the U.S. by Kids Can Press Ltd.
25 Dockside Drive, Toronto, ON M5A 0B5

Kids Can Press is a Corus Entertainment Inc. company

www.kidscanpress.com

The artwork in this book was rendered in cut-paper collage, watercolor,
acrylic and pencil crayon, with some digital assembly.
The text is set in Cambria.

Edited by Jennifer Stokes
Designed by Michael Reis

Printed and bound in Heyuan, China, in 3/2021 by Asia Pacific Offset

CM 21 0 9 8 7 6 5 4 3 2 1

Library and Archives Canada Cataloguing in Publication

Title: My city speaks / written by Darren Lebeuf ; illustrated by Ashley Barron.
Names: Lebeuf, Darren, author. | Barron, Ashley, illustrator.
Identifiers: Canadiana 20200388355 | ISBN 9781525304149 (hardcover)
Classification: LCC PS8623.E2975 M9 2021 | DDC jC813/.6 — dc23

Kids Can Press gratefully acknowledges that the land on which our office is
located is the traditional territory of many nations, including the Mississaugas
of the Credit, the Anishnabeg, the Chippewa, the Haudenosaunee and the
Wendat peoples, and is now home to many diverse First Nations, Inuit and
Métis peoples.

We thank the Government of Ontario, through Ontario Creates; the Ontario
Arts Council; the Canada Council for the Arts; and the Government of Canada
for supporting our publishing activity.

My City Speaks

Written by Darren Lebeuf

Illustrated by Ashley Barron

Kids Can Press

This is our city.

But this is *my* city.

My city moves.

It rushes and stops
and waits and goes.

My city opens and shuts.

It buzzes and tweets
and flocks.

My city grows.

My city is busy

and relaxed.

My city plays

and works.

It walks and runs and climbs and slides.

Sometimes it's smelly.

Sometimes it's sweet.

It pitters and patters

and drips and drains.

It dings and dongs

and rattles and roars.

My city speaks with whispers and giggles and sometimes meows.

My city also speaks with hasty honks, impatient beeps, distant chimes, reliable rumbles, speedy sirens and urgent clangs.

My city speaks ...

and sometimes it just listens.

I wonder what my city
will say tomorrow.